BAD HABITS DIE HARD

BAD HABITS DIE HARD

MALIN HL FORSMAN

Bad Habits Die Hard

www.malinhlforsman.com

Paperback: 978-1-959224-02-0
Hardcover: 978-1-959224-04-4
eBook: 978-1-959224-03-7
Library of Congress Control Number: 2022915449

This is a work of fiction.

Both front and back photos are by Athina Strataki.

Ordering Information:

Prime Seven Media
518 Landmann St.
Tomah City, WI 54660

Printed in the United States of America

I like to thank Ross, who is the inspiration for my main character Rory. We met in Hawaii 1990 and we are still special friends!

CONTENTS

PART TWO

PART THREE

INTRODUCTION

Pamela Andrews is a woman who is a creative author and speaker. She is posh, interesting, and lives a comfortable life. However, her whole world changes when she gets together with a rich and charismatic man with a mysterious past. The man is raised in the shadow of the mob where foul play is part of everyday life. As they say, "Bad Habits Die Hard."

PART ONE

CHAPTER 1

SEATTLE

They met for the first time in Seattle, at the famous Pike Place Fish Market, during a chilly month in February 2015. Rory had just slipped and fallen on the cold icy pavement, the fresh fish he'd bought now annoyingly spread all over the ground. All of a sudden he just laid there on the icy pavement stiff; feeling like an idiot.

Pamela, a famous writer who happened to be nearby, helped the handsome man collect himself and gathered the slimy fish off the ground, putting them back in the sack for this beautiful stranger. That was how it all began.

The beautiful woman helped Rory to his feet and steadied him on the icy surface. She smiled at him and said, "You need different shoes!" Rory was always attracted to the opposite sex but this woman was overwhelming. His dark brown eyes looked deeply into hers. "Tell me, who are you? A superwoman?"

Pamela shrieked, laughing out loud, her voice calming as she spoke "you know, I grew up without a man in my life, so I learned to take care of myself." Rory, still mesmerized by her beauty, stood firmly and asked, "What is your schedule for today? Can I buy you lunch?" Pamela stared at his bag of fish and uttered, "I think it would be too smelly, to be honest."

Rory smiled. "You're right, let's get rid of the fish first." He approached a man in line at the Fish Market and gave him his bag of exclusive fish for free.

He then took Pamela's hand and off they went to a lunch deli. It was so cold outside, so Rory took off his fur coat and placed it around Pamela's shoulders as they walked.

The coat smelled like a *real* man, Pamela thought to herself. Like sandalwood.

Once inside the heated restaurant, they were shown to a table with a view of the dark ocean far below.

The chemistry between them was instant. Their presence sparkled, so much so that people in the restaurant were turning around to gaze at them, wondering who this special couple was. Pamela ordered a glass of Chardonnay and Rory requested a beer. "So, who are you, beautiful lady?" They sat opposite each other, Locked in each-others gaze.

Pamela smiled. "I'm a writer. And what do you do?" Rory ran his hand through his thick curly hair and replied. "By the way, my name is Rory Martin," he said with a low, sensual voice.

Pamela felt a shiver down her spine.

This man was something else. She suddenly felt a wave of emotions. Rory took her hand, and whispered "and what's your name, drop-dead gorgeous?" Pamela started laughing, "You know that is like a high school expression....drop-dead gorgeous...ha ha..." Rory stared at her "well, maybe you're right! But I was the one who fell out there on the icy street, because of your beauty, and I am definitely not in high school!"

Pamela smirked and responded to his touch. "My name is Pamela, after Pamela in the TV series Dallas, my father adored her." And then she laughed and said. "So, I am baptised after Pamela Barnes Ewing, a character in a soap opera."

"Ah, I thought I recognized you!" Rory expressed himself with a crooked smile, waiting for Pam to laugh.

The waiter arrived with their beer and wine. "Well, cheers to you Pamela, you saved my life!" Pamela had to admit that this man was funny. "Actually, I was saving your fish, which are now gone."

Rory burst out laughing "Well, who cares about the darn fish, now that you are here?!"

"So, now tell me, Rory, what is it that you do?"

"I am an inventor."

"Inventor of what, exactly?"

Rory avoided the question, saying nothing he shook his head. "Do you want to have a steak at my place? Now, that we do not have any fish left."

Pamela smiled but thought fast, she did not know him, he could be evil.

"You know, stranger, I was on my way to run some errands." She sipped the last drops of her fully buttery Chardonnay. "But how about dinner later downtown?"

She could not tell if Rory was disappointed or not. His dark eyes shifted into a romantic mood. "Well, I suggest that we meet tomorrow Friday and spend the weekend together."

Pamela felt confused. But she did have the weekend off. And she was the boss of her own life. As a writer, she could write from anywhere and have a free schedule whenever she chose. "What do you mean?" Pamela gazed at this beautiful middle-aged man. He admired her whole persona and almost whispered. "Do you want to hang with me for the weekend? I promise you, I have no bad intentions. I think I may have just met the woman of my dreams. There will be people around us, you do not have to fear anything, I think you are a goddess and would love to get to know you better." Pamela blushed. Rory continued.

"I will pick you up at 2 pm tomorrow outside the Art Museum at the corner; on 1300 1st Avenue." He then took her hand and kissed it seductively. Pamela had to admit that she was falling for him as well. His gorgeous lips lit a fire within her. Before departing, they kissed each other on the cheek and were both filled with anticipation until they would meet again.

Pamela started to walk back to her hotel in the heavy snowstorm, yet she felt like she was flying. It was like she just had had a love injection. The stranger had kissed her hand and cheek, she replayed the moments in her mind. Even though she was in her forties, it was like love had found her for the very first time. Pamela was swept away in her head and physically by this stranger. My God, she thought to herself, should I see him tomorrow?

Pamela noticed that she'd been walking in circles, she was freezing, her feet numb from the cold. She hailed a cab. And finally, a Seattle Yellow Cab pulled over.

"Take me to 168 S Jackson Street, please! The Cadillac Hotel!"

Once back in her hotel room she inhaled deeply and looked around her room, staring at all her books, her life's work. The title of her latest book was: "How to be In Charge Of Your Own Life!"

Is it not ironic, she reflected, one hour with a handsome stranger and she felt like she was not in charge anymore, lust had taken a hold of her.

There was a knock at the door which made Pamela's heart beat faster. "Yeah, who is it?" "There's a package for you Mrs. Andrews!" Pamela opened the door and reached out for her purse to give the bell boy a small tip. She closed the door and opened the package. It smelled like perfume, it was, Angel by Thierry Mugler. There was a handwritten letter on stationery with sensual patterns, which read "I can't wait to see you tomorrow, don't forget about me! Pack a bag with something suitable for warm weather! See U at 2 pm outside the Art Museum. Yours, Rory"

How did he know she worshiped that beautiful scent by Mugler?

Inside the package, there was also a magazine with her face on the cover, that said: "FIND YOURSELF with PAMELA ANDREWS!"

Yes, he had done his research in just a couple of hours and found out where she was staying and who she really was.

Pamela could not help smiling but she also felt slightly uneasy.

Who was this guy?

CHAPTER 2

MATCH MADE IN HEAVEN

Pamela couldn't believe it. She was packing summer clothes into her travel bag, while on her book tour in the state of Washington, during the snowy winter.

Thankfully, she had brought a few summer items just in case she decided to take a detour via LA before flying back to New York.

It was midnight and Pamela had ordered room service two hours ago. And now she had attacked the minibar. She felt like an excited teenager, going out on a date for the first time. It was crazy. She cheered to herself in front of the mirror, staring at herself while thinking this stranger might be the one.

She woke up the following morning feeling anxious and confused. Wondering if she should go through with this date? She took a hot shower and her haze of doubt began to fade. Because she was so excited and it felt right.

After washing her hair and shaving her legs, she put on a robe and called her publisher in New York. It was 3 pm on the East Coast, though still only noon in Seattle. "Tony, it's Pam. I am almost done with the book tour, are we still on for Tuesday and Thursday of next week."Tony replied - "You are phenomenal, they loved you in Tacoma, we have several orders from Barnes and Noble, both there and in Seattle. There's an interview with two local TV stations, KOMO 4 and KING 5 on Tuesday and Thursday you're scheduled to read for the students crowd at the Psychology Department of the University of Washington, so yes-you are still on!" "OK, Tony. Great! So how's the weather in New York?"

"It's worse than in Seattle." "So Pam, darling, what are you going to do with your glorious free weekend?"

Pamela hesitated, should she tell Tony about her hot date? She decided not to. "I'll likely do some shopping and maybe visit a SPA," she said.

They finished their conversation and Pamela shivered. Why was she so nervous?

She put on new underwear she'd recently bought at Seattle's Zovo Lingerie, before throwing on a pair of jeans and a big cozy sweater. Her summer bag was packed. She went to pick up the package which had the fabulous scent of Angel and sniffed it. As well as reading the note from Rory for the tenth time. Okay, she was ready to go into the unknown.

CHAPTER 3

TAKING OFF

Pamela left The Cadillac Hotel, taking a cab to the Art Museum at the corner on 1300 1st Avenue. She paid the driver and stepped out of the car, the cold snowstorm hit her face. "Oh shit! My make-up!" She swore to herself.

Suddenly a man held her shoulders from behind her. "I'm so glad you came!" Rory whispered sensually in her ear.

Pamela felt an explosive sensation running through her entire body. She could hardly speak. She was nervous but excited. Rory smiled when she turned around and faced him while he took her bag. Amusingly he uttered, "I should carry your bags, people might take me for a wimp for not being a gentleman assisting such a beautiful lady." Pamela burst out laughing. "So, where are you taking me, Sir?" Rory answered loudly, "hold on, my driver is here."

They slid into the backseat of his private car. Rory leaned in and kissed Pamela for the first time. It was the best kiss Pamela had ever had. It felt so genuine and lasted forever. This was love at first sight.

Pamela was bewildered as the car entered the VIP area and pulled up to a private jet. She couldn't believe this was happening. They boarded the plane and made themselves comfortable. Shortly after take-off, Rory said calmly "I want you to do something for me!"

Pamela admired the private Jet and then looked deep into Rory's velvet brown eyes.

"What babe?" she asked. Rory pulled her closer to the coach. "Take your clothes off and make love to me!" Pamela hesitated and said strictly. "I will not make love on order! Where are we going, handsome?"

Rory took her hand in his, gently. "I'll tell you soon enough!"

They left a cold and snowy Seattle from Tacoma Airport.

Rory called a personal steward to come out with 2 bottles of chilled Bollinger. "Honey, I know we just left winter land but it's nice and warm here on board. So, let's enjoy some chilled Champagne, please make yourself comfortable!"

A handsome flight attendant appeared with the Champagne, glasses, and some Dole pineapple rings. "So, Pamela, do you want to guess where we are going, the clue is the pineapple!"

"Hm," said Pamela with her hand over her chin. "Well I know a place where delicious pineapple famously grows. If I'm correct, our flight will take approximately 6 hours." Rory laughed. "I knew that you were too bright for me!" Pamela ran her hand through Rory's well-groomed hair and faced him on the comfortable couch. He responded by grabbing her shoulders with his masculine hands. It was a touch of fire. Pamela then out bursted "So, you want me to dance the hula-hula for ya?" Rory grinned and nodded his head. "Well, I can do that sugar! But first, we have to drink A LOT of Champagne!"

"But remember, I'm a very responsible woman!"

The Bollinger was flowing, they kissed and both felt like they were on cloud nine.

"Is this your Jet, Rory?" Rory kissed her neck slowly. "No, I rent it by the hour." And then he grinned secretly and started taking her clothes off. This man was a mystery.

Pamela could not believe that she sat on a private Jet with a stranger she had met just a couple of days ago, tipsy and in her underwear. Pamela moved her gorgeous body in an attempt to do some hula-hula dance. Rory drooled, this woman had it all, he thought to himself. He reached out for Pamela and suddenly they were on top of each other, like excited rabbits, feeling each other out ready to make love. Rory's sharp tongue discovered her vagina for the first time, slowly and thoroughly; he treated her clitoris like a ripe and delicious fruit. Pamela shivered with delight, she climaxed, her body swept up in a hurricane of pleasure. Rory's erect penis pressed firmly into her wet pussy, exploding them both into orgasm. It was erotic and long-lasting, and they both felt high on love.

They landed at Honolulu airport several hours later, however it felt like a joy ride that ended all too fast. It had been a thrilling fantasy that Pamela never wanted to end. Rory made her feel like a goddess.

They had landed in paradise and Pamela had changed into a summer dress and looked sensational.

Yes, she felt on top of the world. Pamela had been in love only once before, despite being well over forty. It was with a neighborhood boy back in Rhode Island in the eighties. Since then she had other relationships but she'd forgotten the feeling of being in love. Her books were her babies and big love affairs. Also, she was loyal to her close friends, she barely gave time to herself.

A driver greeted them at the airport and gave them each a lei around their necks. The red exotic flowers smelled tropical. Hawaii was a piece of heaven and the warm winds comforted them. Pamela could not stop wondering if this was a routine date for Rory?

Over and over again she asked herself who he was? She jumped into the back of the limo and sat close by Rory's side. She felt a burning sensation just being next to him. Pamela had honestly never felt like this before.

She bit her lip and whispered to Rory. "So where are we going, superman?"

For once, he gave a proper answer. "I have a beach house in Kailua and I think you will love it!"

CHAPTER 4

The Beach House

Pamela woke up early the following day. She looked at Rory in the huge bed next to her, he was sleeping like a baby. She grabbed her tunica from her carry-on bag.

Then she went directly out onto the beach just in front of the solid oak porch. Hawaii was phenomenal! The house was gorgeous, it all felt surreal.

The sunrise made her feel like she was in heaven, she pinched herself and thought she was dreaming. Besides Pamela, there was only one couple further away on the beach minding their own business.

The golden sand felt cool between her toes as she walked barefoot towards the shore. Who could imagine that the winter book tour would take a detour to the summer paradise of Hawaii? Pamela enjoyed every second in the tropical climate.

The water was like a turquoise lagoon. She dropped her tunica and swam out naked. It was pure heaven. Pamela loved to swim and Hawaii was inside-out satisfaction for the mind, body, and soul. Feeling the warm and salty water on her skin she felt so lucky.

Like a mermaid, she came up from the water and happened to hear a scream that affected her whole being. It was a dreadful, gut-wrenching scream. Pamela rushed out of the water and fought to get into her tunica. It wasn't easy, because it clung to her wet body. She then ran towards the beach house. Eventually, she entered the door and came into the house.

She noticed blood on the rug. Pamela panicked and shouted "Rory?? Are you okay?" A maid was sitting trembling on the floor in the living room. "What happened?" Pamela cried.

The Hawaiian girl stared at her. "He's dead, he's dead!!! You can't go in there!"

Pamela pushed past the girl and opened the bedroom door. The bright, coastal interior was now overshadowed by terror. Remains of a body lay over the bed. The face was unrecognizable, but she knew it was Rory. The sheets around him were soaked in blood. She could feel her gut-churning.

"Have you called the police?" Pamela desperately called out to the young maid. The maid sat frozen, trembling without answers. Pamela pulled out her phone and called 911. Trying to describe the beach house's whereabouts to the police. Then she went to the bathroom where she fainted and fell hard on the bathroom floor.

CHAPTER 5

TROUBLE IN PARADISE

Pamela awoke, anxiety deep in her chest, she could hardly breathe. She was lying on a bench out on the patio of Rory's beach house. A man leaning over her said firmly, "You'll be okay ma'am! I'm Michael Kim from the Honolulu Emergency Services Department.

Here with me is Nolan Williams from the Honolulu Police Department."

"You made a phone call to 911 this morning, reporting a murder. But all we found here when we arrived was you and a proper and empty beach house."

Pamela couldn't believe her ears, was this all a nightmare? "We wonder if you smoked too much weed last night?" Pamela shook her head desperately. "I was here with my new man in my life and went out swimming and when I came back there were blood prints everywhere." "And a maid was sitting and crying and told me he was dead." Pamela sobbed hysterically. Nolan looked like Magnum the PI, he assured her that there were no traces of criminal activity at the house. Nothing was bloody and no maid. He looked seriously into Pamela's eyes. "The owner of this house is Mr. Rory Martin. We've not been able to contact him to verify your story." Pamela sat up furiously, "Of course not, I told you, he's dead. I saw him, chopped up like an animal, there was blood everywhere." She burst into tears, in a state of shock, her chest was heavy with pain. "Okay, Pamela? We have searched the property, including your luggage. We believe you are a writer Miss Andrews. We want to get you all the help you need and make sure you feel safe here. The paramedic will give you some pills, to calm your nerves. You should get some rest. We'll help you inside. Here's my card, if you feel unwell please don't hesitate to contact me. We can arrange for you to see someone at a local hospital." Pamela sat up straight again and managed to convince the Policeman that she was okay. She felt awful inside but she knew she didn't want to go into a psychiatric ward, that would be even more terrifying. "And ma'am here is one package of Diazepam 10 mg and another with 5 mg." Michael Kim, from the Honolulu Emergency Service, gave the two packages to her and explained. "Take the stronger ones for a couple of weeks and then you continue with the 5 mg, if you still don't feel 100%, please contact me." Then Mr. Kim gave her his direct number.

Pamela watched as the authorities left the property and wondered what the hell was going on. Was she going crazy?

She went inside the beautifully cleaned-up beach house and found some cold Chardonnay in the fridge. She poured herself a large glass. Pamela shivered. Mentally she was in hell, but physically she was in paradise. Then she took one pill of the Diazepam and swallowed it with a big gulp of wine. What had just happened? My God, she had seen Rory dead, brutally killed in the master bedroom. Why was there a maid at the crack of dawn?

Pamela realized she still had the wet tunica on, which was partly dry now after several hours. She knew she could have not been passed out for such a long time. The Police had probably other things to do than babysit her.

Pamela brought the wine glass with her into the bedroom where she stared at the bed. It was all made up of crisp, fresh sheets. Not a single stain of blood. It was all a mystery. Pamela finished the wine and went into the kitchen for another pill and more Chardonnay. Without it, she thought she would go nuts. Thereafter she went out onto the porch again and slouched heavily onto the couch. She noticed that the beach was much busier. There were windsurfers out in the bay and people walking along the shore. Families were enjoying themselves on the beach, and children's laughter made the picture even more idyllic. But Pamela herself was in pain. She knew that she should take a shower and call her publisher Tony. To keep her mind straight and pull herself together.

But then she passed out again and her wine glass shattered into pieces on the patio wooden floor, as she fell into a heavy sleep.

CHAPTER 6

THE CALL

Pamela woke to the sounds of crickets and had forgotten where she was. The ocean kissed the beach with a calm, healing sound effect. My god, she was in Hawaii. Still at Rory's beach house.

She felt like she had been hit with a bulldozer. She slowly tried to get up off the couch. It worked but she was a bit unsteady. She screamed, she had just walked into the glass pieces from her wine glass. Her feet were bleeding, Pamela tried to get away from it all into the house. Now, there were bloody footprints again in the Beach House. But this time, not from Rory.

Overwhelmed with emotions, Pamela started to cry. Then she fetched towels from the kitchen. And soaked up a towel with tap water and some cleaning liquid.

After rinsing her feet in the kitchen sink, she put some band-aids on her sore feet, which she thankfully found in a drawer. After that, she cleaned up the blood on the floor. It was all exhausting. But somehow she managed. And she was thinking so much that she did not even acknowledge the pain from her tortured feet.

Pamela exhaled and made some fresh coffee, hoping to clear her head. She had found some Kona Coffee in a cupboard above the sink. When the coffee was ready she took a sip and just inhaled deeply. And then the phone rang.

She didn't know if she should answer.

She hesitated for a moment and took another sip of the strong, black coffee. The phone kept ringing…

"Okay, I need to know what's going on" she convinced herself and picked up the receiver.

"Hello?"

A familiar voice spoke her name tenderly "Pamela!"

My God, it was Rory.

"Please, darling DO NOT PANIC! I will explain everything later. Take my car and drive to Diamond Head. I am at a friend's house at 4140 Black Point Road. I can't come by the Beach House right now." He continued and Pamela listened in shock.

"This phone line is not traceable or possible to eavesdrop on, so you are fine."

Pamela whispered, "Rory, what happened, are you okay?" Rory replied he was and that she should pack her bag with all her belongings and lock The Beach House up.

"Do you want me to come right away?" Pamela asked tenderly.

"It's for the best!" Rory said convincingly. "The car key is in the flowerpot outside the bathroom." He continued, "Do you have your cellphone with you?" Pamela was tense and began to realize that she had not used it since last night and she didn't know exactly where it was. "You'll need it! Rory adds, "Search the house for it while I am still on the line."

Pamela took another sip of coffee and started to look around. Slowly remembering it might be in the bathroom, where she had called 911 that same hideous morning.

CHAPTER 7

TOWARDS DIAMOND HEAD

Pamela found her phone in the bathroom, as well as the car keys in the flower pot.

Before locking up the beach house, she took one last look around, knowing she was eager to leave.

After leaving the front door she headed toward the parked car with her bag in her hand.

She approached the huge Dodge Ram in the driveway. Everything felt off. She had been through a thriller-like escapade there in Hawaii. And she still wasn't sure what was coming next. It was pitch black outside but the warm tropical climate made it feel a bit easier.

Pamela managed to start the Dodge, and thankfully it was an automatic gear. She connected her mobile phone to the dashboard and typed the address '4140 Black Point Road' into the car's navigation system. Then, she drove away forcefully, while watching the beach house fade in the rearview mirror.

After some miles, she noticed she was leaving Kaneohe and Kailua. Pamela was going to Honolulu first. She felt better and inhaled the stuffy car air with a relieved attitude, grateful that she'd been able to escape the 'haunted' Beach House. And she anticipated that Rory was alive.

There was a lot of traffic and standing in line was not the finest moment in life, Pamela thought to herself. And she could feel her heart beat faster. To part her thoughts she put on the radio.

The car's internal system was too advanced and hard to find the radio stations.

Eventually, she could hear Elvis' comforting voice on some classical Oahu radio station. It was pure soul food. Elvis could sing like nobody else. The song was *'In the Early Morning Rain'*. Ironically, as she sat there, it began to rain.

"What a man!" she mumbled to herself. Pamela loved Elvis. Suddenly, she giggled weirdly to herself. And she could not stop laughing. Yes, she had gone nuts. Pamela was stuck in a car jam and on top of that in a tropical rain growing into a crescendo of water cascades. The radio announcer talked slowly.

"Aloha, I am Patrick Duane and you are listening to Old Goodies in Paradise." *'You Win Again'* by The Bee Gees started to play.

Pamela sighed as she fell down memory lane. Her windshield wipers were going at a fast crazy speed to make sure she could see through the car window. The tropical rain was pouring madly against the windows. Pamela thought to herself, well it's better the windshield wipers are going nuts rather than me.

Pamela gazed at her cell phone and it was finally fully charged. Rory didn't call, she thought he probably thought her phone was tapped. But she remained calm. The traffic started to run smoothly. After driving through the tunnels she eventually passed a sign declaring directions to the Ala Moana Shopping Mall on-road H1. Directly after that, a sign to the left showed The University of Hawaii at Manoa. Pamela then thought about her arrangements to attend the University of Washington in a few days, she had no idea if she'd ever make it.

The rain had finally stopped. And Pamela was on Hunakai Street, not far from where she was heading. She was nervous all over again. Trying to reassure herself, she spoke aloud "Pamela get a grip! For crying out loud, you are strong, you're successful, you're powerful, you got this!"

CHAPTER 8

Black Point Road

Pamela had arrived, she was on the curb of 4140 Black Point Road, close to Diamond Head. She could see this was one of the finest areas to live at on the island of Oahu. She stepped out of the car and looked around, holding her bag in her left hand.

The front door of the house opened. And there he was, Rory! But his beautiful curly hair was gone, he was completely bold and looked a little different. "Pamela! Come in!" He hugged her tightly. It felt so good. Pamela looked around at this vast, exquisitely decorated home. Rory led her to the sofas in the living room.

Pamela uttered, "Rory, you have to tell me what the hell is going on!"

They sat close together and Rory leaned his legs over next to Pam.

"Darling, I told you that I'm an inventor." Pamela nodded her head. "Well, it is so that I make a lot of money on my inventions."

Pamela frowned and thought again to herself, my God what is this man inventing? "There are some bad people after my patents. They'll do pretty much anything to get hold of this information." he mumbled, "the dead body you saw at the house were parts of a pig. I know it sounds terrifying but I had to fabricate my own death. I'm truly sorry you had to be involved Pamela, I truly thought we'd be safe here!"

Then Rory kissed her magically there on the couch. Pamela felt all that sweet love again. "But if you fabricated your death, why had the crime scene vanished when the Police arrived?"

Rory smiled vulnerably. "As I said before, you are too bright for me!"

They cuddled and made out, deeply and lovingly, she was so grateful he wasn't hurt. After an hour or so, Rory left the couch and looked back at Pamela. "You must be hungry?" Pamela then realized she had not eaten for at least 24 hours. "Let's order pizza!" Rory laughed that contagious laugh of his. "Is it safe to order here?" Pamela understood that Rory was under enormous pressure. "Honey, this house is like Forte Knox. My friend, the guy who owns this villa is high up within the CIA. And I have the right to use his name whatever I do, as well as using his credit card."

Pamela exhaled, feeling a bit relieved. At least Rory had his guardian angels.

After a while when the pizza delivery guy arrived, Pamela went outside to greet him in a cap. It was late and dark but she was still nervous. She paid for the pizza with Rory's friend's credit card. Then she gave the Pizza guy a 5-dollar tip and went inside. "He must think I was greedy, regarding what neighborhood we are in."

After enjoying the pizza they walked hand in hand into one of the bedrooms. Exhausted, laying in each other's arms, they both fell deeply into a much-needed sleep.

CHAPTER 9

Fearless

They woke up the following morning in the comfortable bed, so happy to be together again. On top of that, the Hawaiian sunshine lit up the room magically.

Rory kissed Pamela all over her body. She trembled with delight. His penis got harder by the second Rory went down on her and Pamela climaxed like never before, she wanted their moments to last forever.

After 45 minutes of lovemaking, Pamela took a shower while Rory made breakfast. The water ran through her short curly hair. Every inch of her body enjoyed the shower like it was a waterfall. Pamela was so high on life and so very much in love. So, she sang loudly in the hot shower….."I am ready to take a chance again"… an old happy hit by Barry Manilow.

Finally, out of the shower Pamela entered the open kitchen in a long silk robe she had found in the bedroom, Rory's persona lit up when he saw her, the beautiful day was just starting. "Good morning, I made you a cheese and ham omelet." It smelled fabulous. Rory stared at his beautiful woman. "Do you want me after the food?"

Pamela nodded and hugged him with her whole body. She was handed the plate and she sat down at the table. "So, is pineapple juice okay from the Dole plantation?" Pamela smiled and uttered, "Of course! There is someone else in here who smells very good," she said with a gaze. Rory approached her and pulled her wet hair he kissed her on the neck. Pamela died of satisfaction. She was so in love. It was like being transported to heaven; yes, every moment was exhilarating with this exciting man. "So, you had to shave your head?" She managed to say awkwardly. "I miss your thick beautiful curly hair, stud!"

"Yeah, don't you like it? Well, to be honest, it was Reed, the guy who owns this place, who suggested I should do it."

"And what about the Dodge Ram outside? Is it in your name?" asked Pamela worryingly "Of course not, beautiful!" Rory sat down in front of Pamela at the kitchen table and took a big bite of his omelet. Pamela ate the delicious homemade breakfast with passion. This perfect guy was able to both run the world, make love, and cook.

Pamela's cell phone made a noise in the hallway. "Oh, I guess it is my publisher," She says, "I have upcoming appearances on Tuesday and Thursday."

Rory took a napkin and dried his gorgeous lips. "Well, then you'll have to be there!"

Pamela looked overwhelmed and hesitated. "Is it Sunday?" Rory nodded. "How weird, it feels like we came to Hawaii 6 months ago and it has only gone 48 hours approximately." Pamela was overwhelmed. Rory looked at her and outbursted. "Let's book a plane for tomorrow evening!"

Pamela could not help laughing. "Just like that?" Rory stared at her convincingly.

"Today I have arranged something special for you!" Pamela shrugged and thought what on earth could that be after all that had been going on. "When did you have time to do that?" Rory smiled mischievously and flirted with a wink. "Well, you were in the shower a long time, I have booked us a private Hawaiian Luai."

Pamela questioned, "today?" Rory gently took her hand. "Yes, today! It wasn't easy, a lot of tourists were booked to be there. But you know, everyone can be bought if the price is right." "I don't want you to leave Hawaii thinking about the dreadful things you have been through. Also instead of the regular 5-9 pm Luai, we're going sooner, at noon." Pamela felt happy, "What should I wear?" Rory replied, amused. "In paradise? You should wear as little as possible!"

Pamela burst out laughing.

CHAPTER 10

PARADISE COVE

Pamela and Rory arrived at the seaside Luai in Kapolei at noon. It was beautiful! Seafront with a magnificent view.

Two Hawaiian men and a woman greeted them in traditional Hawaiian outfits.

They gave Pamela and Rory each a refreshing Mai Tai in huge TIKI glasses. The beautiful Hawaiian woman swayed her hips in her hula-hula dress. They all had several leis around their necks. One of the men put a lei around Pamela's neck, made from the most beautifully smelling, tropical flowers.

Rory whispered, "this is a tradition that means 'I love you' in Hawaiian." Rory had a lei placed around his neck. Then they were shown to a table for two. Rory grinned, telling her "they will soon serve us some spectacular Hawaiian dishes." The sky was an intense blue and the sun was shining, they were at this gorgeous place called Paradise Cove. Hawaii was absolutely a paradise on earth.

Rory cheered for his woman. "May I have a dance?" Pamela drank up her Mai Thai and obeyed willingly.

Rory took his strong hands and folded them like a glove around her tiny and delicate hands.

They moved tightly together towards the incredible beach spot. Once there Rory kissed her passionately. Pamela was love-struck. Rory then walked her down to the beach, closer to the ocean, where no one could see them. "Here?" Pamela hesitated. "What are you up to, stranger?"

Rory laughed and lit up a marijuana cigarette. "This will help you relax, now when you do not take the calming pills anymore. "Pamela took a deep drag and started to giggle after several inhales. "Hey you!" she exclaimed "Mr. Rory Martin, Mr. mystery!" Rory held her in his arms while smoking. And then he sang surprisingly in her ear, "*Wise men say, only fools rush in, but I can't help, falling in love with you!*"

Pamela felt like her whole life had reached nirvana. Following the sensation, they all of a sudden could hear the beating of drums coming from the nearby stage; where the Hawaiian show would entertain them.

"I guess we should attend our show," Rory whispered sensationally into Pamela's ear. She felt like a teenager and followed his act, whatever he wanted them to do she was all into it.

They got back to their table, the only front row seats. And they were served many different Hawaiian exotic dishes. Pamela thought it tasted okay, she would not say anything but she preferred Italian food or some spicy Thai. The drinks kept flowing. They were both mesmerized by the show, in total awe of the hula and fire dancers, they were phenomenal. All of the dancers represented different traditional dancing moves from each of the 8 Hawaiian islands. The beautiful women portrayed The Big Island, Maui, Kauai, Niihau, Oahu, Molokai, Lanai, and Kahoolawe.

Pamela felt like a Queen with her King sitting there watching it all. The sun eventually began to set and she realized this was the end of her Hawaiian fantasy. They had to go back to Washington State and Seattle the following day.

Rory held her tight and offered his summer jacket on her shoulders. "So, tell me where are you originally from my darling, Pamela?"

Pamela cuddled up beside him at their special place in front of the stage. The dancing was over and it had gotten darker. But candles were lit all around them. Before letting her answer he proudly announced, "I am falling in love with you Pamela!" Pamela pretended not to hear and answered,

"I'm from Rhode Island, I went to school at Brown University in Providence." Ross rapidly followed up, "What did you major in?"

The chemistry between them was one in a billion. Pamela looked lovingly at Rory, now that his adorable hair was gone, she could observe his total beautiful features. "International relations and affairs." Pamela whispered as a reply to his question. Rory smiled and said," I bet you have had a lot of affairs with *your* beauty!" Pamela blushed, laughing out loud. "And your family?" he asked. "My mom was born in Sweden and she met my father at the age of 16 while visiting a relative in New York City. They fell in love and married three years later. I was born in the peek of the hippie era, back in 1969, I'm the only child. So, I was quite spoiled."

Rory took a sip of his last Blue Hawaiian drink. "You know Pam, I think I've had enough coconut Hawaiian punch for one night." Pamela laughed and replied, "Me too, stud!" Rory made a phone call and twenty minutes later a car arrived to take them back to Black Point Road.

CHAPTER 11

HEADING BACK TO SEATTLE

Heading out of Paradise Cove, In the back seat of the burgundy Lincoln, there was a gift wrapped for Pamela.

She felt like a child on Christmas morning. "Rory, you spoil me rotten!" Rory smiled while his incredible eyes penetrated her whole system. "Because you are worth it!"

In the gift box, there were four perfume bottles. There were her absolute favourite perfumes in the world Giorgio Beverly Hills, Poison, Organza, and Angel.

"Rory, it is kind of frightening! How do you know me so well?" He smirked, "Well, I do my research, babe!"

Suddenly a call from Rory's cell phone broke the playful atmosphere. Rory picked up his phone and was listening carefully to everything being said on the other line. When the conversation was over the whole warm atmosphere was gone. Pamela stared at Rory "What's going on?" Rory acted troubled, sitting silently beside her in the back seat. "Reed called, the dodge RAM has been targeted at the house." "What do you mean by being targeted?" Rory sighed "We have to leave the island immediately. There have been some unwelcomed visitors at Reed's house and there has been an explosion in the Dodge. And they have tried to break in into

Reed's mansion." Rory continued with a calm, whispering voice. "A special task force is there now. Our plane is ready to get us out of here right away." Then Rory turned to the driver, "Iwata, head for the airport!" "Pam, do you have all your travel documents and ID with you in your purse?"

"Yeah, I guess Rory." Pamela could feel the turmoil in her brain. She had lately become used to it. It was all just too much to take in.

Eventually, they arrived at the special section at the airport. Where they were transported out to the Private Jet section in only a matter of minutes.

Rory took Pamela's hand and looked deeply into her eyes. "Pamela, you must go back to Seattle alone. I will always love you but I cannot go with you!"

Pamela went nuts. "What are you saying? Are you not coming with me?"

Rory looked serious. "I am thrilled that the roads of our lives were joined by destiny. But I can't jeopardize your safety anymore. This is when we say goodbye, BUT let's do it the Hawaiian way. Aloha, with a lot of love for both hello and farewell."

Pamela felt like throwing up. It was like a crazy nightmare.

Rory kissed her passionately and whispered "Now, you have something to write about! But don't tell for a couple of years, promise?"

They kissed goodbye once more and Pamela boarded the Private Jet alone, in only a light summer dress and her purse on her shoulder. Still wearing the lei around her neck. Although, the flowers had started to whither, like herself.

The pilot introduced himself as Dan, as well as, a flight attendant Cindy who would serve Pamela throughout the trip to Seattle. The plane was soon in the air, but without Rory, It was like a part of her had died.

CHAPTER 12

ALONE

Cindy approached Pamela with Rory's jacket and her perfume bottles. They had been in the air for perhaps 20 minutes. "Miss Andrews, Rory wanted you to have this!"

Pamela laid back in the comfortable leather seat, one that only a private Jet could offer, while smelling Rory's jacket intensely. His natural fragrance about him was enchanting, she shed a few tears and wondered if she ever would see him again.

The flight attendant approached her again." Miss Andrews, we do have some winter clothes that you can have when we are landing in Seattle. Pamela whispered tearfully "thank you so much!" And then she fell into a deep sleep.

Four hours later she woke up due to severe turbulence.

"Miss. Andrews, are you doing okay? The flight attendant said in a soft and carrying voice. We need to take a detour, due to the difficult weather. Is there anywhere else you like to go to on the West Coast? We do not, however, have fuel all the way to make it to the East Coast.

Pamela had an enormous headache and could not think clearly. And she couldn't bare the thought of being in a cold climate again after only just getting accustomed to Hawaii's precious warm weather, so she heard herself announce "Is LAX okay?" Cindy excused herself and said that she would ask the pilot.

Dan the captain called her on the speaker. "Miss. Andrews, so Los Angeles it will be!"

Pamela could not help by laughing a bit hysterically, what was going on in her life? Her life had become like living on a different planet with a new reality.

CHAPTER 13

Shop Till You Drop!

The plane landed in Los Angeles at LAX airport, after 7 hours in the air. Pamela had been drinking water on board as she felt very nauseous, both physically and mentally. She did not have any appetite. It felt she'd lost her right arm being without Rory. A man who had only recently entered her life but he felt like her soulmate from the first moment they had met.

She said goodbye to the crew and managed to make a joke, "I guess I don't need those winter clothes after all." They smiled and wished her good luck.

She had charged her iPhone on the plane but had not checked for any incoming calls.

Her phone vibrated in her purse. It was her publisher, Tony. "Pamela!" Tony was very upset. "I have called you dozen times! I was scared you'd been kidnapped or even worse, killed!" Pamela was walking towards the cab area.

"What If I told you I almost did, you have no idea Tony!"

"Where are you?" He demanded. "I have been in Hawaii for the weekend and I've just arrived in Los Angeles, "she said, sounding out of breath. "My God, what is going on?" Tony screamed down the other end of the phone. "Are you alright?"

Pamela replied calmly. "I'm fine Tony. But you'll have to cancel my event for tomorrow and Thursday in Seattle. I cannot be on the radio right now." "Why?" Tony replied anxiously. "You can take the Red Eye plane this evening!" "NO, TONY!" She exclaimed, "I've been through far too much this weekend to be talking about my books!"

"Okay, okay…I get it. Should I postpone?" Pamela felt like smoking all of a sudden. "I don't know Tony. These two events were the last of the Seattle tour. Tell them, I have the flu! And I will see you back in New York in around two weeks!" "Two weeks?" he proclaimed. "YES! I need a vacation, I think I'm going to go and see a therapist as well!" Tony remarked, "Hawaii is good for the nerves, whatever happened there?" Pam sighed and said stubbornly. "Eventually, I will tell you all about it. And when I've found a hotel here in LA, I will let you know where I'm staying. Speak with our public relations lady in Seattle and get my things and my books out of the room before checking me out of the Cadillac Hotel. If they need my confirmation, tell the hotel to call me!"

Tony, could never understand Pamela Andrews totally, but she was his most successful writer so he just had to hold back and shut up.

When Pamela had finished the conversation with Tony she stopped a cab. It was daytime and it was a nice summer breeze in Los Angeles, instead of the cold winter temperature that ruled in Seattle. At least that made her feel a bit better.

"Take me to Rodeo Drive!" Pamela told the driver.

It took 40 minutes to get there. She announced that she wanted to go to Ralph Lauren on 444 North Rodeo Dr, where she had been several times before. Pamela still just had her summer dress and her purse plus Rory's jacket and the perfume bottles in a bag.

She entered the nice store with the best personal shoppers in the world, she was greeted warmly.

As she'd learned from experience, staff at the most exclusive stores were nice to credit cards and not people. However, she played along with the charade, and it was quite an enjoyable experience. “Welcome Miss! What can we help you with?” “I need several outfits.” she said. “A couple of shirts, some turtlenecks, pants, a pair of jeans, underwear, and blouses. Oh and some shoes also. “The store clerk responded eagerly,” Well you are in the right store and the right place, what is your name, Madame?” “I’m Pamela Andrews and thanks for taking care of me,”

“Sit down in the comfortable coach and I will bring everything you need.” Then the well-dressed man called after his colleague Sarah.

“Sarah, please open a bottle of Champagne for Mrs. Andrews to enjoy while she waits!”

Pamela sat down on the plush sofa and exhaled heavily. Finally, she would get her life together step by step. At least when it came to clothing.

Her phone rang. “It’s me, Rory. Are you okay?” Pamela gasped. “I am in Beverly Hills.” She could not help feeling ecstatic, she thought she might never hear his voice again. Rory sounded cool. “Well, you know, the pilot told me about your whereabouts. I have arranged for you to stay at *The Beverly Hills Hotel* in a bungalow as long as you like. And Pamela, I am sorry for all this horrible experiences, baby!”

The store clerk handed Pamela a glass of champagne while she was talking to Rory. “So, what’s happening to you?” Pamela could hear the shiver in her own voice. Rory hesitated for a brief moment then answered in a low tone.

“Do not worry about me! I leave for Canada tomorrow.” Pamela felt unsure of what to think about everything that had happened. “Will I ever see you again?” she pleaded,

“Of course, Princess! You are the apple of my eye!” Pamela started to laugh. This man could make her feel good. “I miss your kisses, Rory!”

And then they hung up. Pamela felt warm all over and she was ready to shop until she dropped.

CHAPTER 14

THE BUNGALOW

Sitting in the cab on her way to *The Beverly Hills Hotel*, Pamela was surrounded by big shopping bags. After the Ralph Lauren store, she ran over to the "Skincare and Co" and bought everything she needed beauty-wise. From makeup and cleansing products as well as day and night creams.

It felt nice. She cleared her throat. "Driver, can you please stop soon and buy me a carton of Marlboro Gold? You will get a great tip!" The driver stopped at the next gas station and fulfilled Pamela's wish.

Eventually, she was at her destination and let out at the legendary hotel where stars had lived since it opened in 1912 on Sunset Boulevard. However, the real movie stars had moved in there for delightful adventures since during *The Roaring 1920s*. Pamela as a researcher and writer always loved to google the historical aspects of places where she was going to stay.

Pamela paid the cab driver and was instantly greeted by a bellboy who carried her bags as they entered the grand entrance of The Beverly Hills Hotel.

Pamela mentioned to the receptionist that she had been booked into one of the bungalows.

"Yes, I can see that here Mrs. Pamela Andrews, you are booked in our Superior King Room with Balcony. Close to a bungalow!"

Pamela followed along, behind the young boy, who had her key and luggage. She was stunned when the hotel room door was opened. It was fabulous. Certainly, she could live there for a while she thought to herself. She tipped the young bellboy and locked the door behind him. Pamela felt like cinderella. Even if she made a lot of money on her own, she had never stayed at this kind of luxurious hotel in her entire life.

She took her clothes off and wrapped herself in a hotel robe as she filled up the bathtub. And in her gorgeous room, there was a message.

Aloha, my delicious Pamela. Please enjoy your stay! Love, Rory

Once again she asked herself, "who was this incredible guy?"

Pamela woke up an hour later in the bathtub. She must have fallen asleep and she was freezing, the water had turned cold.

However, she managed to get out of the bathtub and then took a long hot shower.

Afterward, she put on the fluffy robe again and walked into her bedroom where she grabbed the unopened carton of cigarettes from her bed. She found some matches in the living room and went out to the veranda and smoked three cigarettes by Marlboro in a row.

It was 4 p.m. on Monday the 9th of February. The rest of her book tour in Seattle had been canceled. She felt guilty. Because she never used to cancel her obligations to her audience and her readers. But at this time of her life, she could just not do it. So, she called down to the front desk.

"Hello, Pamela Andrews here. Do you have a SPA massage available for tonight?" The receptionist forwarded her call to the SPA area of the glamorous hotel.

It was booked, an 80-minute massage by a man called Frank at 7 pm. Then she felt a bit sad and alone, she was missing Rory tremendously. And she did not even have her laptop. Pamela needed desperately to write. Writing to her was like therapy and meant the world to her. How this mysterious stranger Rory could change everything in her life was a big question mark. No, not really because it was pure love.

PART TWO

CHAPTER 15

RORY MARTIN

Rory grew up in Palm Beach, Florida, 'on the right side of the bridge.' He was around 10 years old when he went out to jump into the pool one hot day during the summer of 1972.

What appeared in front of his eyes was a terrifying sight for a young child to experience and of course for anyone. His family owned a small chateau on Clarendon Avenue, in upper-class Palm Beach. Where the high society had held their grand summer parties since the late 1800s and early 1900s.

Young Rory became numb, in a state of shock. His beloved mother was floating in the pool, which had turned red due to the spill of her blood. Rory fell to his knees beside the pool and screamed at the top of his lungs "NO! NO! Mummy!"

His nanny Laura had heard his awful scream, a scream so loud it could make anyone turn cold in despair, she came out running towards little Rory.

Laura was only in her late teens herself and tried to remain calm for Rory's sake. She screamed after the kitchen help while holding Rory. "Call 911!"

Rory's mother Gretchen was found murdered at the age of 28.

After that dreadful day, Rory's life would never be the same.

Rory's father Perry Martin was involved in a drug cartel, since he was 25 years old, without the rest of the Martin family knowing about it. Perry invented the concept of 'wanting more'. He was never satisfied even if he was born with a silver spoon. He didn't really need the extra cash. But for him, it was being addicted to a dangerous game that he could not stop playing.

The hit job of Gretchen Martin was used to scare Perry off. They wanted to hurt him badly for always earning the most amount of *dough*. Perry had fooled his opposition many times. He had been blackmailed for years but never gave in. Perry had also left Gretchen and their son Rory in Palm Beach while he went into hiding in South America.

When Perry and Gretchen got married at the end of the 1950s, Perry had inherited the Palm Beach estate from his parents as a wedding gift.

Their son Rory was born in 1962 and the family was thrilled to have been receiving such a beautiful boy.

However, in 1970 Perry left his family because of all his dangerous liaisons, and he never came back.

Rory has a few memories of his father, the tough guy who was always working.

So, when his beloved mother was killed in the summer of '72 Rory was without parents. He was sent to different boarding schools all over Europe by his aunt Nancy. Rory always ended up in fights and was expelled from one school after another.

At the age of 21, he was due to inherit a lot of money from his aunt and he returned to the USA.

Hurtfully, he had never heard anything from his father who was presumed dead since the early 1970s.

Perry Martin's enemies did not forget about his son. So, Rory was also their target. Rory staged his death several times during the years to come.

Of course ,he was not an inventor which he had told Pamela and many other women over the years. He was filthy rich due to family money. However, he had been chased all his life. And he knew the hunt would not stop until he was 6 feet under.

CHAPTER 16

IN BEVERLY HILLS

Pamela had a lovely relaxing massage the first evening at *The Beverly Hills Hotel's SPA*. The following day she went out and bought a Mac laptop at Digicom situated at 5844 Santa Monica Blvd.

She felt unsatisfied without her writing and she hated writing by hand because her hand would cramp.

She was full of ideas for a new book. This time around it would not be a self-help book that inspired women in their daily lives. It would be a thriller that would scare anyone who read it.

She eventually sat down on her giant hotel bed and thought about Rory. The computer had been loading and was ready to use. The intro to her new book would say: "Was he dead?"

Meanwhile in Hawaii;

Rory was tired of all the lies about his life. How could he ever live normally? There was no way out!

Reed's home had not been in any further danger at Black Point Road. The Red Ram was okay as well. But Rory knew they were after him as always and he didn't want to drag Pamela into his mess any longer. His friend Reed at the CIA had got a warning that Rory was in severe danger.

The Beach House in Kailua had burnt down the day after Pamela had left, but Rory didn't want to tell her, he didn't want to keep scaring her.

Rory was deeply in love with Pamela. She was 46 and he was 53. However, they both appeared younger. How could he get some happiness once and for all? Reed and Rory sat on the back porch looking over Diamond Head, each with a beer in their hand. Reed slowly said out loud, "So, what are your plans this time?" Rory shrugged his shoulders. "My pal, I am soon out of ideas." Reed stared at Rory and replied. "And are you in love?" Rory nodded his bold head and exhaled. "That is the problem! Never fall in love right!" Rory grunted. "Well, Reed, I've had a lot of girlfriends. My first at the age of 14 was at my boarding school in Switzerland. I got a 15-year-old girl from France pregnant and was expelled. After then I decided not to get too attached to a girl again. The loss of my mother was just too much for me to deal with." Reed took a sip of his beer.

"Well, Rory maybe you should comment on this unfair love game on Oprah's network! Come on Reed!" Rory could not help laughing. Without his sense of humor, he would probably have been dead 10 years ago. "So, if you love this Pam of yours, why don't you just stop running and marry her? Get 24-hour security, You are the one who can afford it." Rory put his head in his hands and was speechless. He never thought about the whole enchilada that way. "Well, Reed. You always seem to have a solution but I'm terrified they will kill her." "Rory, you are fucking 53 years old. Do you want to keep running forever? Isn't this woman a writer?" Rory nodded. "Well, tell her the whole story and she can write about it. You might lose your money but you'll have your love!"

Rory thought hard to himself. Could he live like a poor guy, depending on his woman? Would she still love him if he was all of sudden a rag?

The following morning in Beverly Hills

Pamela was awoken by a knock on her hotel room door. She jumped out of bed and slid on the hotel robe and opened the door. A young girl was standing there. "Miss Andrews, housekeeping?" "It's too early?" Pamela mumbled. The girl smiled gently and went away from her room. Pamela was confused, why did they send a cleaning lady at 8 am, when she was staying for an additional week?

She called down to the reception desk. "Pamela Andrews here. Please tell me why you sent a maid to my room at this time? I have been writing all night and need my sleep!"

The desk clerk answered. "I am so very sorry Mrs. Andrews, but we have not sent you a cleaning lady. Are you sure?" Pamela got upset. "Are you suggesting that I'm lying?" Pamela slammed down the receiver with enormous force. Thinking about it, she had actually recognized the young maid. She couldn't get back to sleep and went straight to the bathroom and took a shower. Oh my god, she thought to herself, was it not that Hawaiian girl who screamed that Rory was dead at Rory's Beach House in Kailua?

Pamela felt shivers down her spine. She finished the shower and looked for a towel.

Out of nowhere, right beside her, she heard a male voice say, "Is this what you are looking for?" Pamela's heart jumped a beat. Before she could move a man in a mask threw the towel upon her. She was stark naked and vulnerable. "Who are you?" she screamed. The man in black laughed. "I am here to pick you up, a request from your new boyfriend." Pamela tried to escape to the living room, but the stranger was right behind her. "Put something on before I rape you! I am starting to get a hard-on." Pamela sobbed hysterically. "Damn lady, pull yourself together! We don't have all day!" Trying to focus, Pamela put on her new jumper and pants. She was so scared that she couldn't find her underwear. "Are you done? Do I have to help you pack? You're useless!" The stranger had a deep intimidating voice. He behaved like this was a normal thing to do while he, the crazy person, was two feet away.

CHAPTER 17

KIDNAPPED

A phone rang loudly at the house in Honolulu. Rory was still at Reed's house but Reed was not at home. Rory finally found his phone.

"Yeah?" He says, sounding completely out of breath. A dark voice from the past loudly announced. "Did you like the fireplace in Kailua?" Rory knew instantly that this guy was one of his vicious enemies. One of the ominous children of the mob that had followed him from a very young age.

Rory was silent, he put on the recorder. "Well, Mr. Martin, we have your woman here." Rory's heart fell like a stone.

Nooooo, they had her! He felt sick to his stomach. "So, Rory, you wanna listen to her!?" It was Pamela crying on the other end. "Rory, please help me!" Rory said steadily to the kidnapper. "What do you want?" "I want your money, I want your assets, and if I want I'll fuck your broad for a month straight too, at least she'll be totally satisfied when she gets back to you!"

"No, please! Okay!" Rory shouted, "In exchange for Pamela, I'll give you everything!"

Rory wanted to kill this guy, he was the son of his father's worst enemy.

"I know it's you Kevin?" Rory whispered. Kevin was quiet. "You know Kevin if you even touch Pamela's arm, I will kill you!"

Kevin laughed loudly and cynically. "Well, Rory you are way too late for that. I have tasted her deepest and most delightful treasure!" With that response, Rory hardly managed to stay cool. "You know Kevin, Pamela's a famous author. If the word comes out that she has been kidnapped, you'll have nowhere to hide!" "You better hurry up and pay me then, bald man!" Kevin replied with a smirk on his face.

Rory uttered, "Listen, I'll do whatever you want, just don't hurt Pam. Please! Where are you?"

Kevin hid a big gesture and kissed Pamela's one breast and sucked her nipple very hard. Pamela was strapped upon a bed in the back of a van. She was almost naked and tied up around her wrists.

"Well, dear Pamela, what shall we do with you?" Kevin whispered down the phone.

"You know Rory, your woman is turning me on nicely and I need to be satisfied."

Rory was frozen. He tried to respond calmly, not wanting Pam to get hurt, even if he was totally disturbed and anxious.

"I'll give you 10 million dollars, to begin with. I can get it to you as soon as possible!"

Kevin laughed awkwardly and hung up.

Rory called Reed right away, his hands were shaking. He felt like someone just had hit him in the head and his stomach, at the same time.

"Reed! They have her!" Rory burst into tears like a baby. "Rory, calm down! We will trace the call immediately! I will call my expertise in these matters at CIA." They hung up. Rory stared helplessly for a moment. Then he called The Beverly Hills Hotel.

"Good Evening, welcome to The Beverly Hills Hotel! Please hold!"

Rory was going crazy. Eventually, the receptionist came on the line. "My friend Pamela Andrews has been staying in one of your suites for several days. When did she check out?"

"Pamela Andrews? I am sorry we have had nobody with that name staying with us at the moment." "Well, check harder, she was there, I paid for the hotel room." "Sir, I can't help you if you are rude!" Rory thought to himself, when did all this nonsense start happening at the most exclusive hotels in the world. "Sir, I'm new here, you need to talk to the hotel manager but he's not here today, may I suggest you call back tomorrow!"

Rory was even more furious and felt like he could faint. He hung up and could just wait for Reed to get back to him.

Reed had been in Pearl Harbour with a client but was back at his house just two hours after Rory's disturbing phone call.

Reed jumped out of his car and opened the gate with a code.

He ran into the house where he found Rory wasted after drinking a bottle of whiskey. "You idiot, we can't find her if you are drunk!" Rory slurred. "I will be okay!" And he added, "Kevin knew I was bald." Reed let out a long sigh of despair and punched Rory straight in the face. He went to the kitchen and put ice cubes in a bowl of cold water. "Put your head in this bowl!" He demanded; while Rory put his face into the icy cold water and he held his head down for what seemed like minutes. Rory came back up with a sore face. "Now jump into the pool!" Reed lectured him. Rory was confused but did what he was told to do. He swam under the water back and forth for 15 minutes. Reed made some strong coffee in the open kitchen and went out onto the patio, watching Rory struggle in the pool. "Okay, that's enough! Come up here! I have a towel and some strong coffee."

Rory was a good-looking man with a nice chest. He was wearing only his briefs when he climbed out and grabbed the towel. It was dark outside but the pool was lit up, and they couldn't be seen from anywhere on the patio.

"Rory, hear me out! We have to act smoothly if you ever want to see Pamela again. This Kevin guy is a monster, but you already know that." Rory felt like someone had run over him with a steamroller.

CHAPTER 18

ON THE NEWS

Reed sent Rory to bed and he preferred to sleep on the couch in the living room, despite there were several bedrooms in the house.

Early the following day, Reed had made some phone calls. Rory had woken up after a restless 5 hours of sleep and eagerly wanted coffee.

"Morning, Rory! So I took the liberty to look into your phone records to try to locate Pamela. We have Pentagon involved."

"Hey, Reed! Perhaps they even come after me now." "No, man. Your money is old money by now. What your father made his money outside his wealthy family is not an issue anymore. It is not relevant. His secret was buried with him according to authorities. But this Kevin guy has just tried to scare you all of your life. And you have invested in so many companies over the years. And remember that your aunt's money that you received was family money from real estate."

"I just had to get that off my chest. You are a real friend Reed. But now he has her. My first real love whom I found as a middle-aged guy. I would like to torture him until his last breath!"

"Listen!" Reed put the volume up on the TV set.

The host of Good Morning America spoke. "We have some disturbing news. Tony Gordon, a well-known publisher is with us today. One of his famous clients who is a well-respected author, Pamela Andrews, is missing. Mr. Gordon, what is going on?"

The book publisher Tony took a sip of the coffee they had given him in the TV studio.

"Well, Pamela Andrews was on a tour in Washington State and had to cancel two events, which she never normally does. Pamela is a professional person and she never lets down her readers and fans. I am afraid that something horrible has happened to her."

Reed muted the TV while Rory got restless on the couch.

"My God, Reed, it's all over the news! They even showed her picture!"

"Rory, calm down, this could be a good thing!"

"Reed, we need to find her!"

Reed took a deep breath. "Look, we're waiting to hear from the CIA, thank God I still work for them part-time these days or they'd be no help at all."

Reed's phone rang and he looked at Rory. "This might be them!" He put the speaker phone on.

"Reed, Daniel here! We think we have a trace on them, the kidnappers and Pamela Andrews are on their way to Mexico in an old Volkswagen bus."

"How'd you find them?" Reed asked passionately.

"We've had eyes on Kevin Nicholson for over a decade. He's always managed to walk away, he has had too many connections, you know the drill. But if we can get him for kidnap and murder we can finally put him away."

"What about the writer, Pamela Andrews?" Reed challenged.

"We'll do our best Reed, but I can't make any promises." And then they hung up the phone.

Rory felt sick to his stomach. It was all his fault. He knew it could be dangerous, bringing Pamela into his life, what on earth had he been thinking? It was a nightmare. If it all ended badly he would never forgive himself.

CHAPTER 19

TIJUANA, MEXICO

Pamela woke up shivering on the bed she was still tied to, in the back of the filthy Volkswagen van. She felt nauseous after the drugs they had given her. She was half-naked and had no recollection of the last few hours.

She sobbed as the van was slowing down and eventually came to a stop.

The back doors opened. A small, stocky man was standing there, dressed in black, a mask over his mouth. "Okay, famous writer, welcome to Mexico *guapa*!" He spoke with an accent. "Get dressed, we're gonna be here for a couple of days." Pamela had severe anxiety, she felt like her hope of surviving this was growing smaller by the second. "Come on girl" Kevin approached the van, "are you not satisfied after the kinky sex we had last night?" Then he laughed viciously out loud. "Your pussy was so wet, you begged me to go down on you and fuck you hard. I know you liked it!"

Pamela felt sick. She was in hell and prayed relentlessly that she would be saved. Then Kevin released Pamela from the bed and threw her some clothes. She was too weak to fight, she felt like a zombie. She was living a nightmare.

She stumbled out of the van beside Kevin, He whispered in her ear, "Stand up and behave now, we're on our honeymoon remember!" He clutched her arm and held her tightly next to him, grinning as they walked. The sun was shining and the temperature was hot. Some people they met on their way to the hotel did notice them and smiled.

After a short walk, they reached a cheap motel. They entered their room and Kevin threw Pamela down onto the horrible bed. "Okay, honey! I'm gonna give you a little vitamin shot. So, just relax and enjoy the ride!" Pamela felt she'd probably be better off dead at this point. Kevin placed a needle into her vein and she instantly felt motionless. She wondered if it was heroin. But just thinking of that it scared her tremendously. After a while, she felt high and dozed off.

Kevin got a call on his cell. "Ferry! The news!"

"What channel?"

Ferry Duncan was a criminal bad boy and had worked for Kevin for over 8 years.

"Pamela Andrews' disappearance is public. Her publisher has been on Good Morning America."

Kevin was furious. "I'm gonna kill that son of a bitch!" Ferry whispered, "It is too late Kevin! You've got to get Pamela out of that motel now and we need to disappear."

CHAPTER 20

A Plan

Rory's hair started to grow out and he felt like a punk rocker with this buzz-cut look. However, he didn't give a damn. Pamela was on his mind 24/7 and she was the only thing that mattered to him.

Reed had done all the groundwork he could to get hold of the kidnappers through his connections within the CIA.

While Rory had organized his private plane firm to take them to Mexico. Reed and Rory were both heading for the Honolulu airport by Uber. They had hardly had any luggage.

"Rory, you know you don't have to fear these guys anymore, they will be caught!"

Rory replied smoothly, "It's easy for you to say, Reed! You know my beach house was recently burned down."

"You are not a criminal Rory! You have no issues anymore regarding your money and taxes. This guy Kevin was brought up to believe that your father tried to fool his father. He is bloodthirsty and a lame character."

Rory sighed and put his head in his hands. "Reed, he has Pamela! I would kill him or myself to save her life. And what about that pig we had to kill to stage my death?"

Reed coughed and asked the driver, "Is it okay if I smoke? The anxious driver nodded his head against his will. "Rory, we will get her back alive!" But honestly, Reed had never felt more uncertain. "I just hope you're right Reed!"

They boarded the jet and headed for Mexico.

Meanwhile, Reed's partners at the CIA had arrived in San Diego. Four tough guys who have managed to bring down some of the most notorious mobsters and murderers over the years.

CHAPTER 21

32 HOURS

Ferry Duncan and Kevin Nicholsen carried a heavy sleeping Pamela Andrews back into the van.

"Okay, Kevin. Let's go to Acapulco!" "How long will it take to go there?" "Around 32 hours," Ferry replied. "We need to make some demands to Rory. Make him put the first 10 million dollars into Pamela's account and she'll transfer it to your offshore account!"

"Ferry, he is a billionaire. Why only make it 10 million?" "Oh that's just the start, my friend!" They both chuckled mischievously. "Okay, Ferry. Let's hit the road!"

Pamela was tied in the back of the van again. She was still drowsy from the drugs.

They drove like crazy for 6 and a half hour straight. Eventually, they stopped in Hermosillo.

Where they decided to stop for food and stretch their legs. They had smoked joints in the van during the whole journey and the whole vehicle smelled like marijuana. Eventually, they found a quiet place in Hermosillo and parked the van. Kevin went back to look at Pamela. She was awake. "Sugar, do you need some water?"

Pamela nodded. "Ferry and I will get a bite to eat, we'll get take away food for you. Doesn't that sound good?" Then he picked his nose and laughed. Pamela was going nuts. But she was too weak to respond and faded away.

Meanwhile back in Tijuana

The CIA men had spoken to the motel owners in Tijuana and asked if they had seen Pamela Andrews. They went to Hotel Suiza and Aqua Rio Hotel. A local informer had given them a tip.

However, they got no answers. The staff was probably bribed. "So, boss, where are we heading?" One of the CIA agents said out loud. Boris, who was in charge of the four of them and was the one who knew Reed well, took a deep breath. "Call headquarters and get them to do another background check on Kevin and Ferry. Every tie they have to Mexico, I wanna know about it. We believe they have connections to property here, a place that we've been after for years. This time we're gonna get it!" "Kevin Nickholsen has been infamous to the drug cartel since he wore diapers! His father was a powerful man and he made no mistakes in taking after him. The police and CIA had been chasing him for three decades but he always managed to slip through their fingers. Kevin had the underworld at his disposal."

Boris told his colleagues in the car, "It's time to reel in this ugly fish!" And off they went toward Mexico City.

Several miles north, Kevin and Ferry stopped at a gas station. They always used cash, so they wouldn't be traced.

Kevin shouted to Ferry, "Fill the van right up! I'm gonna check on the lady in the back. She'll be no good to us if she's dead."

Although she wasn't, Pamela felt like she was dead. She still had not been given any water or food, and her mind was playing games with her because of the heavy drugs.

Kevin opened the back doors of the van once again. "Okay, honey, papa is here! What do you need?" Pamela didn't make a sound. She was trapped in her own body and also in her mind. If hell existed, this was it, she thought to herself.

CHAPTER 22

NO FUN IN ACAPULCO

Reed told Rory, "Boris and his squad are on their way to Mexico City right now. They've been able to track Kevin in Tijuana but he's being protected by the mob."

"So, where do we go from here, Reed?" Rory asked desperately. They were still on board the Jet from Hawaii. Rory felt thirsty for whisky, but he knew he had to stay sober for Pamela's sake. They couldn't make any mistakes this time. It was literally a matter of life and death, Pamela's life. Rory felt like crying like a baby. This woman had struck a chord within him that he never had felt before.

"I suggest that we head for Acapulco" Reed announced.

"Why Acapulco?" Rory wondered.

"Well, Acapulco is long gone from its heydays, today the city is run by the mob, if they're heading anywhere with Pamela, I bet it will be there."

Worried, Rory nodded. "Yeah, I've heard about some of the things that happen down there."

2 hours later

The plane landed at Acapulco airport, they grabbed a rental car and headed straight for a hotel in the middle of the city of Acapulco.

They arrived at a popular hotel, a couple of miles from the center. "Rory, I've heard of this place, it's a 5-star resort, called Las Brisas. We will have our own pool and a separate spot from everyone else. Rory could not help start laughing."

"We're not on our honeymoon old guy!"

"Well, we need to lay low. Money talks here and I will tell them that you are a far-fetched blood relative to King Kamehameha IV of Hawaii, no one will approach us." "Get out of here, Reed! I didn't know you were such a romantic historian!"

Reed paid for the most prestigious penthouse suite. He gave the hotel piccolo a big tip when they arrived at their room.

Rory and Reed had only one bag each with them. Whilst they sat silently in their top floor suite, staring at the most incredible view, Reed's phone rang and broke the silence. Reed starred at Rory. "It is our CIA guys!"

"What have you got?" Reed nodded talking on his cell and looked relieved. Rory was so nervous he had to get something from the minibar. Reed finished his conversation and hung up. "Okay, big guy. Just one drink!"

Rory had already poured himself a gin and tonic.

"So, what's happening?" Rory asked as he paced the room. Reed replied with a stoic face. "They've traced the van." Then, Rory took a big gulp of his drink. "So, what's next? I'm scared to death that Pamela is already gone, that they have killed her." "Come on Rory, without her, they can't negotiate."

"Well, maybe they've hurt her, tortured her, my beautiful Pamela." Rory began to sob. "Get a grip, Rory! Boris has informed me that they are close. It won't be long now!"

Rory took a deep breath. "So, what do *we* do?"

"Boris wants me to alert more people within the agency to be ready for a big drug shipment that's leaving Acapulco tonight. They have ears on the inside. So, you and I will be here, on standby."

Rory felt awful. "I want to be there among Boris and his guys when they get to the van!"

"You know it's too dangerous Rory, you are way too emotionally involved! Plus if they see you they could bust the whole operation!"

Rory frowned. "Okay, okay, I'll stay at the hotel, but you have to promise me they'll get her here as soon as possible." Reed agreed. "However, she might need medical attention right away!" Rory felt like he had just been hit by a car. While Reed focused. "I'm gonna meet the guys soon enough, you stay here and lay low, wait by the phone. I will call you as fast as humanly possible!" They then sat there for a while going through the detailed plans of the operation led by Boris. After a half-hour, Reed left Rory in the hotel room. Rory thought to himself if there ever was a more difficult moment to stay sober. He'd always had a problem with alcohol but somehow been able to lead a moderate and healthy lifestyle, until now. He took some white wine from the minibar and went out to the pool in his briefs. The sun set had appeared. He thought it would be refreshing to lay around in the pool. Rory's hair had grown out fully. But this time it was grayish, because of all the stress. He said a quiet prayer for Pamela and jumped into the water.

MEXICO CITY

Reed was joining Boris and the guys downtown Acapulco some hours later. He was an experienced CIA agent who had been part of the rescuing team for over 35 years within the agency. After receiving the demand for the 10 million dollar ransom, They organized a fake transaction to be sent to Pamela's account. A transaction that would appear legit to the untrained eye. Kevin and Ferry parked the van in the worst part of town and made plans to flee to Brazil as soon as the money was transferred.

"Kev, I think this woman is dead!" shouted Ferry as he stood at the back doors of the van, staring at a lifeless Pamela. In a panic, Kevin rushed to join him, "OMG, no! no! She can't be! She's our ticket out of here. They'll never send the money if we can't prove she's alive!"

Kevin seemed to be just thinking of his worst enemy and swore over the asshole Rory. His mind wandered and he hardly heard Ferry complaining about Pamela.

Reed and his team were closing in on Kevin and Ferry. They were monitoring their conversations from a short distance away. Reed and Boris decided it was time to move in if they were to get Pamela out alive.

They parked in an alley nearby. They waited patiently for their opportune moment. Meanwhile, backup had landed in Acapulco and was on the way to their location. They were about to prevent one of the biggest stings in modern history to succeed.

Pamela could hardly breathe, she could hear Kevin and Ferry arguing about how to get her out of the hot, airless van.

And then the shots began. Kevin and Ferry dropped dead in a blink of an eye. They fell on the asphalt close to the van.

Reed ran to the vehicle and jumped straight in. Then he untied Pamela's wrists and held her tight, "I got you, you're safe now. It's over! The paramedics are on their way, you are gonna be okay!" Pamela finally felt a bit hopeful and relaxed and as a result, fell out of consciousness.

Meanwhile, Rory was so nervous he could hardly handle it. He paced in the hotel suit back and forth after being too restless to stay in the pool. And then the call came. "Reed here, we got her! She's in the hospital, Pamela was in pretty bad shape." Rory whispered, "is she going to be okay?" "We were right on time." Reed reassuringly replied. "Things took a turn, Kevin pulled a weapon and they were both killed on site." Rory felt the weight lift from his shoulders. For the first time in a long time, he felt free.

Reed didn't mention to Rory that Pamela had been drugged. He knew it would be a difficult time for both of them after what they'd been through, but she was alive, and that's what mattered.

PART THREE

CHAPTER 23

THE RECOVERY

Rory was so thankful that Pam was alive and safe. He rushed to the hospital straight away. He was asked to sit in the waiting room while Pamela was having some tests. He waited anxiously and desperately in love with her.

It was 2 am and Rory woke up on the couch in the waiting room. “Reed?” Reed all of a sudden sat there next to him. Then Rory shot up and waited for Reed to talk. He explained that Pamela was fine, telling him she had been drugged numerous times during her kidnaping, so she needed to stay in the hospital a little while longer. Worried but relieved, Rory turns to his friend “Hey Reed, I can’t thank you enough for what you’ve done for me and Pam.” They sat there silently together till the following morning.

Pamela woke up in a pile of sweat. At first, she had no idea where she was. She was trembling and felt nauseous, her body was withdrawing from the drugs. She was scared. A nurse came into her room. “Senora, I am not so good at English. But I will try to explain to you.” Pamela tried hard to focus. “We, have given you some medication, it will help cleanse your body from the drugs you were given. But it may take some time.” Pamela managed to whisper, “will I be okay?”The gentle nurse took her hand. “Yes, you got to us just in time. Is there anything I can get for you?" Pamela shook her head but wondered about Rory.

A nurse approached Rory in the waiting area, telling him Pamela was doing well but that she needed her rest, he would be able to see her very soon.

Reed fetched them both coffee and Rory paced the room.

A few hours later, he was allowed to visit her. He took a deep breath before entering the room where she was staying, his heartbeat was fast. And there she was. He was shaking seeing Pamela lay there in the hospital bed, helpless. Rory was aware that he had to show his strongest side even though he was in shock.

Then he sat down in the chair by her side. "Pamela!" He took her hand in his. She looked at him, troubled. "My darling, I'm so sorry for everything" Pamela shook her head gently, "Rory, it's over. They are gone now." Rory squeezed Pamela's hand firmly and comforting. "I would never have rested until I got you back."

"How are you feeling?" Pamela sighed. "They are giving me medication to help my body fight off the withdrawals from the drugs." Rory felt so guilty.

"Are you hungry?" he asked. Pamela gave him a weak smile and nodded. Rory laughed. "Honey, that's a great sign. I will let the nurse know. I'll be right back!"

CHAPTER 24

IN NEW YORK

Tony Gordon, the publisher of Pamela Andrews, was scared and could not believe what had happened to his *star writer*. However, her book sale had gone up through the roof since his announcement that she was missing, on the TV show *Good Morning America*. Pamela Andrews was now a top seller on the New York Times bestseller list all the way.

Tony sat at his desk, staring out over Madison Avenue. He let his mind wander, he felt guilty for sending Pam on tour alone. He wondered if any of this would have happened if he'd been there with her. He opened a cabinet where he kept a bottle of Jack Daniel's whiskey and poured himself a large glass.

Then his work phone rang loudly throughout his quiet office. Each time it rang he felt his spine freeze. He feared the worst, news of Pamela's death.

There was no staff in the Literature House on a weekend. He was all alone. Eventually, he picked up the phone.

He said slowly, "Literature House here, Tony speaking." Tony could hear someone breathing heavily on the other side of the phone. "Tony Gordon?" "Yes!" Tony whispered terrified. "Can we meet tomorrow, I have some information on Pamela Andrews."

"Who is this?" Tony demanded. The voice responded, "I work for Kevin Nickholsen, he and his partner were killed in Mexico. Kevin was the one who kidnapped your writer, and if you want to see her again you'll bring 50,000 dollars in cash tomorrow."

"How do I know Pamela is alive?" Tony tried to act tough while gulping his whiskey. "How did you get her here from Mexico?"

"Hey, less questions old man! If you want to see her again DO NOT play with me!" Tony silenced. The vicious stranger uttered, "Pamela Andrews is here with me in the Bronx!"

"Okay, okay, where and when shall I meet you?"

"At 4 pm tomorrow at The HOG PIT, 37B W 26th street! Bring the money in a Duffle Bag, I'll know when you're there." Tony hesitated for a second. And then the phone line went dead. Tony shivered and poured himself another big glass of whiskey. He thought about calling the police because he realised that he must be watched. But he didn't want to jeopardise Pam's safety. Maybe he shouldn't have gone public. However, it was too late now.

Tony swallowed the last gulp of the whiskey trying to steady his nerves. And then the phone rang again. "Liberty House!" Tony managed to say in a fake sober tone. On the other end of the line, he could hear Pamela Andrews.

He immediately sat up straight in his chair. "Pamela, is that you?" Pamela answered warmly. "Yes, Tony it's me. I'm safe. I have just been discharged from a hospital in Mexico. I'm flying back into New York tonight." "Oh my God Pamela, what happened? Thank God you are okay, I've been on the news about you. I've been so worried!" Tony stammered. "But wait, there is something else. A guy just called me here at the office, claiming he had you in an apartment in the Bronx. He demanded a ransom from me, I am going to meet him tomorrow afternoon." Pamela said in a soft, calm voice, "Tony there's someone here I want you to talk to, a very good friend of mine, Rory. He saved my life!"

Rory took the phone. "Mr. Gordon!" Tony replied, "Yes hello Rory, I am so grateful to you for helping Pam, I was just explaining to her…" Rory interrupted with his masculine tone, "I heard every word, Tony. I need you to tell me everything this weird guy said, okay?" Tony explained that he worked for a Kevin Nickholsen. Rory interrupted again. "What was the guy's name?" Tony felt like an idiot when he heard himself saying. "I have no idea, but I have the time and place where we are supposed to meet tomorrow. He asked me to bring 50,000 dollars in a duffle bag and said he would know when I was there."

Rory managed to stay calm and asked Tony where the address was. "At 4 pm at 37B W 26th street!" "Okay, Tony, stay calm. Do not contact anyone. Stay where you are. We are leaving Mexico for New York tonight, I will contact you when we have landed!"

CHAPTER 25

CHIP - THE UNHINGED

Chip sat alone at his studio in the Bronx, getting high on cocaine. He felt proud of himself, scaring the shit out of that moron book agent. He had stalked Tony Gordon for several days now since he went on national television. He knew he had the money to pay a ransom and came up with a plan. Chip didn't know Kevin Nickholsen and Ferry Duncan but had heard through a drug connection that they were hit in Mexico and knew that was his chance. As far as Tony knew, Pamela was still at the hands of the kidnappers, and he was going to use this to his advantage. Or so he thought.

Chip had grown up in a bad neighborhood, his mother was a prostitute and his father was an abusive alcoholic. When his father's abused went too far, he was 19, he shot his father. However, he was never prosecuted. Chip had been lucky to stay out of prison. His mother was moved to a mental institution soon after Chip killed his father. He was 28 nowadays, a broken soul with no money and addicted to drugs. He fought with his mental demons daily. Struggling with his addiction he was in a lot of debt. He saw an opportunity with Tony, he wanted to take the money and disappear, start a new life. It finally looked like lady luck was on his side.

The apartment was filthy, cockroaches were all over the place, and a torn piece of dark fabric covered the only window.

Chip gulped bad moonshine and with a smile on his face he passed out dreaming about the following day. A day that could change his miserable life.

CHAPTER 26

THE BIG APPLE

Several hours later Rory's pilot got a clear sign from the JFK air tower, they were finally preparing for landing after circling over the city of New York for almost an hour. JFK was located 16 miles southeast of downtown Manhattan, and they would get there by a private driver. It would take approximately an extra 45 minutes.

Pamela's apartment was waiting. She felt thrilled despite all of her painful experiences. And the best out of this trip was Rory, and he was with her. Her body was aching but she was strong and all of her was on her way to being healed. Pamela squeezed Rory's hand in the back of the limo. He placed his arm around her to give her comfort. "Darling, I'm so glad I have you back!" Rory whispered in Pamela's ear, "I would have given anything, done anything to have stopped all those awful things happening to you, I should never have left you at the beach house!" Pamela felt warm and safe being close to Rory, she never blamed him for anything that happened. They started to kiss softly and passionately. Then the driver asked Rory abruptly, where they wished to go. Rory whispered to Pamela, "Where's your apartment? I want to get you home safe and I will head straight to Tony!" Pamela tried to fix her hair and replied. "It's 121 Madison Avenue, in the heart of Gramercy Park, not far from

Tony's office." Pamela looked intensely at Rory and said. "I'm not sure I want to be alone tonight." Rory turned to face her, lifting her chin with his hand. "I promise I'll be right back, I need to check in on Tony!" Rory held Pamela tight in the back seat.

The car finally pulled up outside her building. Rory took Pamela's hand, and the few bags they had with them in his other. Pamela still felt fragile. And Rory could sadly understand her devious hardship. They approached the doorman who looked pleased to see Pamela. "Good evening Edward!" Pamela uttered. "Welcome home Miss Andrews!"

Rory helped Pamela to the elevator with their bags. She pressed the elevator button that would take them up to the top floor. Rory was impressed when they entered the front door and walked into her lavish apartment. She lived in a 3-bedroom penthouse with a huge terrace.

Pamela started sobbing with relief, she was so happy to be in the comfort of her own home again. Her apartment was her safe haven, and she had written two of her best-selling books there.

"Your place is beautiful, Pamela darling!" In response she sighed, "Thanks, it's not perfect, but it is my home." then she walked to her window and looked out over the bustling city. "I must go" Rory announced. Pamela turned to him and kissed him on the cheek. "Please be safe my love and hurry back to me!"

Rory nodded, kissed her back, and headed for Tony's office.

CHAPTER 27

The Hog Pit

Pamela watched Rory from the window while he was leaving, already anticipating for his return. Looking for something to calm her nerves, she went to the fridge and poured herself a glass of wine after opening a bottle of Chardonnay. She fished through her handbag for the pills she had been given back in Hawaii. And then Pamela swallowed two pills with a big gulp. Afterwards she slumped down on the couch in the living room. And she tried hard not to replay the trauma of the last few days in her mind. Pamela inhaled deeply, closed her eyes, and finally dozed off.

The next morning she woke up on the sofa. She'd been covered with a blanket. Confused and realised she was home in New York and that it was already morning she jumped to her feet. Rory called out for her from the kitchen. He was there and making coffee. "Rory!" Pamela smiled, happy to see him. "Where's Tony, is he okay? What happened last night, why didn't you wake me up coming back?" Rory made his way towards her and kissed her on the forehead. "Tony's fine. He spent the night at his office. I scoped the place out before I left. I'm meeting him this morning to figure out a plan. I didn't wanna wake you, you needed to get some rest." They sipped their coffee. Rory could see the despair in Pamela's face. "Listen, darling, I don't want you to worry about today, I've contacted Reed and he has organised for three of his guys to help us out. I've dealt with guys like this my whole life, this twisted Bronx guy is just trying to make a quick buck. I promise I'd die before I ever let anything happen to you again!" Pamela nodded with teary eyes. "You know Rory, somehow, I think God only gives us as much as we can handle." Then he hugged her tightly.

At Liberty House, Tony barely slept. He was so nervous about that coming afternoon. He wasn't someone who grew up tough, he came from an intellectual privileged background and wasn't accustomed to dangerous situations. He felt like a big baby, wanting to be held by his mother. And despite all evil, he was not allowed to drink until the mission was over. He was the one who was going to mingle with the crazy 'Bronx Man' and give him the Duffle bag filled with 50.000 in dollar bills. Pamela's Rory had called around 10:30 am and let Tony know about the plans after they had meant late last night.

A few hours later

It was three o'clock pm and Rory arrived at the office to get Tony. They were also met by the professional men Reed had sent.

Meanwhile, Chip 'the Bronx Man' was preparing himself in his studio. Through some connections, he had managed to book a flight to Colombia, that was going to take off that same evening. He had his passport and a quite big carry-on bag with a few things. He was confident that he could pull the whole thing off, in a few hours he would be free to start his new life.

Reeds men were not in uniform, and they were in an undercover vehicle and followed closely behind Rory and Tony.

It was almost 4 pm and they parked up a few minutes walk from 'The Hog Pit' where they were going to make the exchange.

The professional men went over the plan once more. And Rory was told to stay in the van, while Tony was fitted with a wire and prepped to follow instructions. He was sweating profusely.

Rory looked him in the eye, "You can do this, it's almost over!" Tony grabbed the Duffle bag filled with paper pretending to be dollar bills. Two of the agents were already inside the restaurant, which made Tony a little less nervous. The third officer followed from a close distance. Tony was trembling and felt like he could faint any second.

He stepped inside the restaurant with the Duffle bag in his hand. He looked around and just froze, only inches from the main entrance. "An agent spoke reassuringly in his ear piece, telling him to stay calm."

Chip the unhinged spotted Tony instantly. He stared at Tony from a table in the corner. Chip then briefly hesitated but eventually made his move. He snatched the Duffle bag from Tony's grip and ran out the door. Tony became frozen, grateful to be alive. He was in shock. The agent who was waiting outside, shot Chip in the shoulder as he ran. Chip immediately fell down, while pulling a weapon from his coat and then he fired back. Then one of the other Secret Service officers who was coming running out of the restaurant shot Chip in the head, so the madness was over.

CHAPTER 28

THE AUTHOR PAMELA ANDREWS

A few days later, Pamela and Rory sat in her living room, drinking chilled Champagne. They celebrated the end of the horrific journey they had been through. Tony, her publisher was fine, he was a little shaken up but that didn't stop him from going back to work the following day. Pamela had always admired his commitment to his job.

Rory gazed lovingly at Pamela "So, when is the next book tour?" She giggled and answered. "You know, I think I'll wait a while before the next one. In fact, I might take a leave of absence for a while, plus, I think I have a pretty good idea for my next story." They chuckled as Rory topped up her glass. "I hear you darling, loud and clear!" Pamela smiled vividly, "Rory" and then she paused. "How do you feel about moving in here with me?" Before he could answer she interrupted with a smirk, "Then you'll always know where I am."

Rory placed his hands on her face and kissed her softly.

"You know, beautiful, it sounds perfect, let's seal that with a kiss!"

www.ingramcontent.com/pod-product-compliance
Lightning Source LLC
Chambersburg PA
CBHW030415310726
48979CB00002B/419

* 9 7 8 1 9 5 9 2 2 4 0 4 4 *